I0548154

The Backpack

original story by Jennifer Degenhardt

Translation by Sydney Bartholomew

For Amy, my oldest friend.

CONTENTS

ACKNOWLEDGMENTS

A huge thank you to my niece Sydney Bartholomew for using her stellar language skills to translate this book for me. Of course I was delighted that she would complete the task, but the real reward was when she thanked me for the opportunity, as she said she enjoyed the different contact with the Spanish language.

Thank you to Chloe Bushaw, a junior at Franklin High School in New Hampshire for the beautiful covers. I continue to be giddy every time I receive a different interpretation. This time was no different.

Chapter 1
Oscar

My name is Oscar Rodríguez. I am thirty (30) years old. I'm not tall, but I'm not short. I'm not fat either, but I am really strong. I have brown eyes and black hair.

I live in Dodge City, Kansas. Originally, I'm from Medellín, Colombia. Now I live in the United States because there are more economic opportunities here.

In Medellín I have a big family: my parents, my two brothers and my sister. My mother's name is Lupe and my father's name is Román. My mom is fifty (50) years old and my dad is fifty-five (55). My brothers' names are Carlos and Javier. They are twenty-two (22) and eighteen (18) years old. My sister's name is Catarina, and she is fifteen (15).

Now I live in Dodge City with my two cousins. My cousins are the sons of my Uncle

Roberto. He is my father's brother. My two cousins and I have a painting company. We paint houses. The company is called Rodríguez Painting. We paint a lot of houses in the town and nearby. It's a good business.

My cousins are also from Medellín. Miguel is the younger one. He is twenty-four (24) years old. He is short, so he is responsible for painting the lower parts of the houses. My other cousin is older. His name is Luis and he is thirty-one (31) years old. He is the tallest one, so he paints those parts of the houses. I am the owner of the company, so I am in charge of the contracts, but I paint too.

When I am not working, I like to watch soccer, and cycling. Sports are very popular in Colombia. I play soccer on Sundays with my cousins and other guys. I also watch a lot of soccer on TV. I don't have a bike in the United States, but I do like to watch cycling races on TV.

I like living in the United States, but I also love Colombia. The two countries are different.

Chapter 2
Michelle

My name is Michelle and I am thirty-four (34) years old. I have blonde hair and green eyes. I am short, but I am really strong. I like to go to the gym.

I don't live with my parents or my sister. They live in Reno, Nevada. My whole family lives in Reno. I live in Las Cruces, New Mexico. I live there with my husband, Marcos. He is forty (40) years old and he's originally from Mexico. Marcos works as a manager of a Mexican restaurant in Las Cruces. Marcos likes food a lot and he likes to cook.

I also work. I work for FedEx. I transport packages and letters from Las Cruces to many different parts of New Mexico, and other states, too. I like to drive because I get to listen to music and audiobooks.

I don't have children, but Marcos has two daughters from his first marriage. They live in Ascensión in the state of Chihuahua, Mexico with Marcos's mother. The older daughter is thirteen (13) years old and the younger daughter in eleven (11). The girls want to come live in the United States with us. They want to go to school in Las Cruces.

I like my life with Marcos, and I like to visit Ascensión, but I want to live as a family with my husband and his daughters.

Chapter 3
Oscar

Dodge City is not very big with 27,000 people, more or less. But I love living here. The people in Kansas are very nice and they work very hard. The main industry here is meatpacking[1].

There are many places in town: supermarkets, pharmacies, museums, a library and many schools. And every summer there is a festival. There isn't a lot of action in Dodge City, but I like it.

My cousins and I live in a gray house. It's not a modern house; it's an old house with three bedrooms. There is also a garage for the van. The rent is cheap.

We have one van for work. In the van

---

[1] meatpacking – where animals are killed and their meat prepared to be sold.

we have all of the materials we need to paint. We paint six days a week. We work every day except for Sundays. On Sundays we relax.

Every morning my cousins and I go to a restaurant for coffee. The restaurant is called Wyatt Earp Coffee. In the restaurant we always talk with our friend, Charlie. Charlie works in the restaurant.

"*Buenos días mis amigos*," Charlie says in Spanish.

"Hello Charlie," I say, "How are you?"

"*Estoy bien, gracias.*" Charlie says, smiling. Charlie likes to practice speaking Spanish.

Charlie serves us three coffees.

"Here you go."

"Thank you, Charlie," I say.

"Oscar, do you need another van for

work?" Charlie asks.

"Yeah. We have a lot of houses to paint and only one van," I tell him.

Charlie says, "My brother has a van that he wants to sell."

"Really? For how much? Where is it? I'd love to see it," I tell Charlie.

"The problem is that he lives in San Antonio, Texas," Charlie says.

"How much does he want for the van?" I ask him.

"He's selling it for only a thousand dollars," Charlie says.

"That's a great price. And we need another van," I say to Charlie.

"You need to go to San Antonio. Is that possible?" Charlie asks.

"Yes. I'll go in a couple of days. On Thursday. Thank you, Charlie."

"No problem," says Charlie.

I talk with Luis and Miguel about the trip to San Antonio.

"I will go on the bus," I tell them. "You guys will need to work. And when I return we'll have another van."

We're happy. We have a lot of work, but we need another van. This is a great plan.

Chapter 4
Michelle

It's Tuesday and I need to drive to San Antonio. It's an 8-hour long trip. I need to bring some special packages to El Alamo in San Antonio.

El Alamo is an important place with a lot of Texas history. In the past Texas was a part of Mexico, but the people wanted their independence. There was a big battle in El Alamo in 1836. That battle was really important for the Texans, the people from Texas.

Now El Alamo is a national park. Many people visit the park to see the mission[2]. The mission has a museum, a chapel and a store. It's a very popular place for tourists in San Antonio.

---

[2] mission - a religious camp/outpost established by the Spaniards following the conquest.

That morning Marcos and I prepare to go to work.

"Marcos, I need to go to San Antonio today. I'll be back tomorrow," I tell him.

"Okay, Michelle. Do you have a good book to listen to?" he asks me.

"I do. Are you going to talk with Deisy and Laura tonight?" I ask him.

"Yes. And with my mom. I need to talk to her about the documents."

"That's good, Marcos. Good luck. See you tomorrow."

I give my husband a kiss and I leave for San Antonio.

My husband Marcos is a good person. He works a lot in a restaurant. He uses the money from his job for his daughters and his mother in Ascensión. Marcos and I visit his family a lot. The trip is only two and a half hours, so it is not a difficult trip, but it is hard when we return to New Mexico. His kids, Deisy and Laura, want to go back with us but that's not possible. This is a typical conversation we have when we leave Ascensión:

"Daddy, when are we going to live with you and Michelle?" asks Laura, the older one.

"Yeah, Daddy. We want to live with you guys," says Deisy.

"Soon, girls. Soon," says Marcos.

It's a difficult situation for Marcos and me. We want to live as a family in the same house.

Chapter 5
Oscar

It's Thursday. Luis, Miguel, and I are in the van. We go to the bus station on Central Avenue in Dodge City.

"Are you ready, Oscar?" Miguel asks me.

"Yeah. I have clothes, my phone, money, and my green card[3]," I tell them.

The green card, or permanent resident card, is very important. After living in the United States for ten years, I finally have official documents. I am now a permanent resident.

"Good. Good luck. See you on Saturday," Luis says to me.

---

[3] green card - permanent residence card; issued to immigrants who have completed the process to be in the United States legally.

I walk in the station and look for the right bus.

I don't have a lot in my blue backpack: two shirts, underwear, and socks. And of course, a toothbrush. The trip to San Antonio is not long, not like the trip that I made to the United States. I traveled with the same blue backpack ten years ago.

The backpack was very important to me during my trip to the United States. And now it's even more important because it has my phone, money, and my green card.

I get on the bus.

I sit next to a young man. He has brown hair and brown eyes and is wearing a military uniform.

"Hello," he says to me.
"Hello," I say to him. "Nice to meet

you. I'm Oscar. Are you going to San Antonio?"

"Yes. My family lives there. How about you?" Dave asks.

"I'm going to San Antonio also. I am going to buy a van," I tell him.

"That's a long way to go to buy a van, isn't it?" Dave asks me.

"Yeah. But they're selling it for a good price."

Dave asks me another question, "Are you from Dodge City?"

"No," I say with a smile. "I am originally from Colombia. I've lived in Dodge City for ten years."

Dave tells me that he has a friend from Colombia. "He's from Medellín," he says.

"I'm from Medellín too," I tell him.

Dave and I talk for a long time. I talk a lot about Medellín and he talks about San

Antonio.

Medellín is a big and beautiful city. The climate is mild. It's not hot, but not very cold. It is a modern city with universities, industry, and festivals.

"I really like Medellín," I say to Dave.

"What do you like best about the city?" Dave asks me.

"In Medellín there are many museums, parks, and libraries. It's a city, but life is very calm," I explain.

Dave is very curious. We talk a lot. I ask him about San Antonio as well.

"Dave, it's my first time in San Antonio. I am going to be alone for a day. Where do you recommend I visit?"

"Oscar, you need to visit El Alamo. It's pretty and it has a lot of history."

"Great. Thank you. Now I'm going to

rest a bit," I tell him.

"Sounds good. I will, too."

After the 10-hour trip, we finally arrive in San Antonio.

"Thanks for talking with me, Oscar"

"Thank you, Dave," I say to him. "Take care."

I'm going to buy the van tomorrow in the afternoon, so first I'll going to a hotel for the night.

Chapter 6
Michelle

In the FedEx truck the air conditioning is on high. It's really hot in the month of August in New Mexico and Texas. I have packed bottles of water and fruit for the long trip. I'll be driving to Fort Stockton, Texas, first. There I'll use the bathroom and take a break for a bit in Pepito's Cafe. It's a casual restaurant with great Mexican food.

The drive to Fort Stockton is four hours. I listen to music on the way. I like country music, especially music by Tim McGraw. He sings the song "Humble and Kind" in Spanish. In Spanish the song is called *"Nunca Te Olvides de Amar."* It's so beautiful.

The trip to San Antonio is really long, but that's normal. In New Mexico and Texas, trips that are five or six hours in the car are typical. On Route 10, after leaving behind the traffic in El Paso, I then pass though many small towns: Socorro, Fort Hancock, Sierra Blanca, y Van Horn. Some of the towns have Spanish names because that area of the United States used to be part of Mexico.

Mexico. The country of my Marcos and my daughters, Deisy y Laura. No, they're not my biological daughters, but they are my daughters. They should be with us here in the United States. Marcos's mother as well. She is old and taking care of two adolescents in the house is a lot of work.

The towns on Route 10 are similar to the town of Ascensión, where Marcos's family lives. Ascensión is close to the border of the United States in the state of Chihuahua. It's not far to travel there, but in reality, it's very far away. We need to submit official documents so that we can have the girls and Marcos's mom live with us. Marcos and I always talk about that.

"Deisy, Laura and your mother need to be living with us in the United States, Marcos," I tell him.

"Yes, Michelle. I agree. We need to find a lawyer," Marcos says to me.

"Good, then. We'll call a lawyer," I say.

"We can't, Michelle. It costs a lot of money."

That's a problem. Submitting the documents is one problem and the money is another.

Chapter 7
Oscar

Today is the day I get to buy the van. I call Charlie's brother.

"Hello. Wally? It's Oscar," I say

"Hello, Oscar. Are you coming to get the van?"

"Yes. This afternoon at 5 o'clock. Is that okay?"

"Of course. I'll wait for you at the house."

"Good. Thank you, Wally."

I have the whole day free. I want to go to El Alamo, but first I take a walk on the Riverwalk in San Antonio. It's a well-known part of the city, especially for tourists. It's a park that also has stores, restaurants, art, and much more along the San Antonio River. It's a place where there aren't any cars. I like visiting the Riverwalk and it's very pretty, but I also want to go to El Alamo.

I walk towards the entrance. I have my backpack because I am not returning to the hotel. I need to keep my backpack with me because my wallet is in it along with my money and my green card. The green card is so important.

I like this part of San Antonio. There is newer construction like along the Riverwalk, but there are also old structures like El Alamo.

El Alamo is a museum. There I learn a lot about the battle, independence, and the history of Texas. It's interesting. After walking a few hours there, I buy a bottle of water.

I am on a bench outside drinking the water when I see a couple of young women. They are really pretty. They have long, dark hair and green eyes. Maybe they are sisters.

One of them says to me, "Hi. Can you tell me where you bought the water?"

"Hi. I bought it in the store," I say.

"Thank you."

They enter the store and return with bottles of water, for them and one for me.

One of the women gives me one. "Here," she says to me. "It's really hot out."

"Thank you," I say back. "It sure is hot. Are you from here? Is it always this hot?" I ask.

"Yes. We are originally from San Antonio. My name is Sandra, and this is my sister, Isabel."

"Nice to meet you. My name is Oscar. I am not from San Antonio, obviously," I say to them, smiling.

After talking for a moment, Sandra asks me, "Do you have plans for this evening? Do you want to go for a walk with us?"

"I have an appointment at 5 o'clock…"

I get my backpack and take out my phone to see what time it is. "…but I have time. Where are we going?"

"Our family's restaurant. We'll take you. It's great. Come on!"

I am excited to go to the restaurant with my pretty new friends. I am so excited that I forget about the backpack and leave it behind under the bench.

Chapter 8
Michelle

After eating and relaxing in Pepito's Cafe, I drive the four hours more to get to San Antonio.

On the way I think about Ascensión even more. The town is small. It's in the style of a Spanish colony with a pretty town square with a church and some restaurants. It's not big and there isn't much to do there. And, it's in the desert and it's hot. There are many more opportunities in Las Cruces for my daughters. But without money, the girls won't have those opportunities. We need to find a lawyer.

I arrive at El Alamo before rush hour. I take the important packages and I go directly to the office. Before I arrive at the door, I see a blue backpack under a bench. I take it with me into the office. But first I look inside.

Chapter 9
Oscar

Sandra, Isabel and I walk to the restaurant. We talk about San Antonio, about our families and the weather. Suddenly, I say, "Oh no! My backpack! I left it at El Alamo!"

I don't have my backpack. My money, my license and my green card are in there. Oh no!

"I need to go back. The backpack is really important," I say to my new friends.

"It's okay, Oscar," Sandra says. "Don't worry about it. Let's go back."

The two women are so nice. They repeat, "Don't worry" many times. But I am not calm. This is a disaster. Of course, I need the money, but my green card is even more important.

We arrive at El Alamo and we go to the bench where I left my backpack. It's not there.

Oh no!

"Let's go to the office and report the problem," says Isabel.

"Yes," says Sandra. "Let's go."

"Good afternoon, sir. I left my backpack on a bench here twenty minutes ago. Do you happen to have it?"

"No, I'm sorry. I don't have a backpack here. Can you describe it?" he asks me.

"Yes. It's an old, blue backpack. Inside there are two shirts, underwear, and socks and also, my wallet. The wallet is the most important. It has my money and my identification."

The man writes it all on a piece of paper. "Okay, Mr. Rodríguez. We will call you if someone returns it."

"Thank you. Thank you very much," I say to him.

*****

I am very sad and worried, but Sandra and Isabel are very nice.

"Don't stress, Oscar. It's okay. Let's go eat at our restaurant."

"We can call my uncle too. He is a police officer," Sandra says. "He can help you."

We walk three blocks to a Mexican restaurant. In the restaurant we talk and eat a lot of food such as corn tamales, chorizo, chilaquiles and more. Afterwards, Sandra calls her uncle.

"Oscar, I called my uncle. He will help you," Sandra says.

"Thank you, Sandra. I need to call the man who owns the van. I can't buy it now because I don't have money," I say to them.

I leave the restaurant and I call Wally.

"Hello, Wally? It's Oscar. I have a problem."

I tell Wally everything and he says, "That's a big problem. No problem. Call me when you find the backpack."

"Okay. Thank you, Wally."

I go inside the restaurant again. I am really worried.

Chapter 10
Michelle

Again, I am driving in my FedEx truck. I have the backpack which I should bring to the office at El Alamo, but I am tired. I decide to stay in a hotel for the night before I return to Las Cruces. Besides, I need to go to the office at El Alamo to pick up a package going to Fort Stockton in the morning. I will take the backpack then.

Finally, I have a chance to look in the backpack. Inside there are two shirts, underwear, socks, and a wallet. In the wallet there is a driver's license, a green card and money. A lot of money.

I count the money: $1200. That's a lot of money. Money that Marcos and I need. I think of the money that we need for the lawyer.

I also think about the residence card. It belongs to an Oscar Gerardo Rodríguez who lives in Dodge City, Kansas. He's not from the United States. He's an immigrant just like my Marcos. Still, Marcos and I need the money.

What do I do?

I think a lot while I drive to the hotel. The hotel is a bit far from El Alamo and it's rush hour so there is a lot of traffic. I am worried. Marcos and I need the money, but I think about Oscar Gerardo Rodríguez. He has to be worried as well. I am going to call Marcos when I am in the hotel.

*****

Marcos has lived in the United States for nine years. His family is from Mexico, but he has more extended family in New Mexico too. In the past, the southwestern part of the United States was part of Mexico. After the

Mexican American war, the two countries signed a treaty and the United States gained a big part of that territory. Marcos has family both in Mexico and in the United States because of the war and the new border between the two countries. Incredible. And still his family is separated.

Marcos already has his legal documents to live in the United States. Now we need documents for his daughters and his mother. It's a very difficult legal process. Because of that we need money for a lawyer.

*****

At seven o'clock in the evening I call Marcos.

"Hi Marcos. How are you?"

"I'm good, Michelle. How was your day?" he asks me.

"Interesting. I have twelve hundred dollars that I found in a backpack."

"What? How?" Marcos asks.

I tell my husband about the backpack, the money, and the green card. But I am tired, so we don't talk for very long.

Chapter 11
Oscar

It's nine o'clock in evening. We are lot still talking and eating, and I am still very worried. But I am calmer when I talk with the young women's uncle.

"Oscar," he says to me. "What's wrong?"

"I have a problem, sir. I lost my backpack and in it I have a lot of money and my residence card," I tell him.

"That is a problem, yes. Tomorrow I'll go to the office at El Alamo. I'll ask about it."

"Thank you very much, sir. I need the money to buy a van for my company."

"What kind of company?" the uncle asks me.

"My cousins and I have a painting company. We paint houses in Kansas."

"In Kansas? Where? Sandra is going to live in Kansas," the uncle said.

"We live in Dodge City," I say.

"Wow! Sandra is going to work in a school there in August."

Sandra? The humble, kind, beautiful woman who has been so nice to me? She's going to work in Dodge City in a few months? No way! But I don't show my feelings then. I just say, "How interesting."

I like Sandra. She is a very nice woman. She's funny too. We talk a lot during dinner.

"This food is from southern Mexico. It's spicy. Do you like it?" Sandra asks me.

"Yes. It's excellent. I like it a lot. But you're not eating a lot. Do you not like it?" I ask her.

"I like all Mexican food, but I don't like chilies."

"But chilies are delicious!" I say with a smile.

"Not for me. Because of that my family says that I am a 'bad Mexican'. Ha!"

"That's not true Sandra. You are a good Mexican," I say smiling. "You're going to work in Dodge City, right?"

"Yes. I am going to be an elementary school teacher there," she tells me.

"I also live and work in Dodge City."

"Seriously? That's incredible!"

Sandra and I spend the night talking. I almost forget about my problem.

Suddenly, my phone rings.

"Hello, Oscar?"

"Yes, it's me," I say.

"My name is Michelle. I have your backpack."

She doesn't say anything else to me because in that instant my phone stops working.

No!

Chapter 12
Michelle

I talk to Oscar for a minute, and suddenly there's silence. What happened? I call him again. He doesn't answer.

I call him two more times and nothing. I will call him again tomorrow.

I watch TV in the hotel and I think about my family. Marcos and I have the name of a lawyer who will be able to help us when we have the thousand dollars to pay him.

I look at the backpack. Well, now I have the money. But it's not mine.

Chapter 13
Oscar

We find a charger to charge my cell phone. It charges, but it's too late. I decide to call Michelle in the morning.

*****

At seven thirty in the morning, I call Michelle.

"Hello, Michelle?"

"Yes. This is Michelle," she says.

"It's Oscar. Do you have my backpack?"

"Yes."

"Fantastic! Thank you! Where are you?"

"I am at a hotel. But I need to go to the office at El Alamo today," she tells me.

I speak quickly. "I will meet you at the office at whatever time you tell me to."

"Sounds good, Oscar. I'll be at the

office at nine," she tells me.

"Excellent. And thank you so much, Michelle."

I am very excited. I call Wally immediately.

"Mr. Wally? It's Oscar. I found the backpack and the money."

Chapter 14
Michelle

I talk with Marcos again that morning.

"Michelle, it's not our money. Yes, we need it, but it's not a good idea to keep it."

"True, Marcos, but how are we going to get the money?"

"Don't worry, Michelle. We'll get the money somehow."

I get in my truck and drive to El Alamo. I want the money, but I don't want to steal from another person. I want to live with my daughters and my mother-in-law, but I don't want to take someone's money to do it.

At El Alamo I see Oscar immediately. He looks the same as in the photo on the green card, but today he has a big smile. He is with other people, two women and a police officer. Is there a problem?

"Hello, Oscar," I say. "I'm Michelle."

Oscar looks at me and looks at the backpack. He is very happy.

"Nice to meet you, Michelle. And thank you very much."

"Here is the backpack. It has everything: the clothes, the money, the license and the resident card. And the charger for the phone."

"The charger! Ha!" Oscar says.

I don't understand why he's laughing. I am still very worried about the police.

"And the police?" I ask him, a bit nervous.

"Oh no, don't worry. He is my friends' uncle. He was helping me with the problem."

"Oh! Good."

Oscar takes out the wallet and counts

the money. He takes a part of the money and offers it to me.

"Michelle, this is for you. For being honest."

"Wow! Thank you, but I can't..." Michelle says.

"Please. These documents are more important than the money."

Sandra is happy too, but she asks me, "Oscar, don't you need the money to buy the van?"

"Not now. This morning I talked with Wally, my friend Charlie's brother. He wants to give me the van for nothing."

"Wow, Oscar. That's terrific!" Sandra says.

"Yes. This whole experience is incredible. There are some good people in the world."

I turn to the group and say, "This is so

great! My husband and I really need the money to pay for a lawyer. My daughters still live in Mexico with their grandmother. Now we can think of a new future. Thank you, Oscar."

"Thank you, Michelle," he says to me.

"Excuse me, but I need to call my husband," I say to them.

Chapter 15
Oscar

I am very happy. VERY happy. I have my backpack with the money and my identification, and Wally gave me the van. I also met new friends here in San Antonio.

"Oscar, when do you have to return to Dodge City?" Sandra asks me. "Can you spend another day with us?"

"I am going to get the van this afternoon, but I can spend another day here," I say.

"Good," she says to me with a smile. "There are other places to visit, if you want. You like history, don't you?"

"Yes, of course."

And I like you too, Sandra. But I don't tell her that.

Not yet.

ABOUT THE AUTHOR

Jennifer Degenhardt taught high school Spanish for over 20 years and now teaches at the college level. At the time she realized her own high school students, many of whom had learning challenges, acquired language best through stories, so she began to write ones that she thought would appeal to them. She has been writing ever since.

Other titles by Jen Degenhardt available on Amazon:

La chica nueva | La Nouvelle Fille | <u>The New Girl</u>
La chica nueva (the ancillary/workbook
volume, Kindle book, audiobook)
Chuchotenango
El jersey | <u>The Jersey</u> | *Le Maillot*
La mochila | <u>The Backpack</u> | *Le sac à dos*
Moviendo montañas
La vida es complicada
Quince | <u>Fifteen</u>
El viaje difícil | *Un Voyage Difficile* | <u>A Difficult Journey</u>
La niñera
Fue un viaje difícil
Con (un poco de) ayuda de mis amigos
La última prueba
Los tres amigos | <u>Three Friends</u> | *Drei Freunde* | *Les Trois Amis*
María María: un cuento de un huracán | <u>María María: A Story of a Storm</u> | Maria Maria: un histoire d'un orage
Debido a la tormenta
La lucha de la vida | <u>The Fight of His Life</u>
Secretos
Como vuela la pelota

@JenniferDegenh1

@jendegenhardt9

@puenteslanguage &
World LanguageTeaching Stories (group)

Visit www.puenteslanguage.com to sign up to receive
information on new releases and other events.

Check out all titles as ebooks with audio on
www.digilangua.co.

www.ingramcontent.com/pod-product-compliance
Lightning Source LLC
Chambersburg PA
CBHW031903170626
46807CB00004B/1876